Find Your Sport

Lisa Greathouse

Consultant

Gina Montefusco, RN
Children's Hospital Los Angeles
Los Angeles, California

Publishing Credits

Dona Herweck Rice, *Editor-in-Chief*
Lee Aucoin, *Creative Director*
Don Tran, *Print Production Manager*
Timothy J. Bradley, *Illustration Manager*
Chris McIntyre, M.A.Ed., *Editorial Director*
James Anderson, M.S.Ed., *Editor*
Stephanie Reid, *Photo Editor*
Rachelle Cracchiolo, M.S.Ed., *Publisher*

Image Credits

Cover Luc Sesselle/Dreamstime.com; p.4 Lightspring/Shutterstock; p.5(top) Sean Locke/iStockphoto; p.5(bottom) Monkey Business Images/iStockphoto; p.6 Joshua Hodge Photography/iStockphoto; p.7(left) Joshua Hodge Photography/iStockphoto; p.7(right) Joshua Hodge Photography/iStockphoto; p.8(top left) Joshua Hodge Photography/iStockphoto; p.8(top right) MedicalRF.com/Photolibrary; p. 8(bottom) MedicalRF.com/Photolibrary; p.9 Shutterstock; p.10 Doug Berry/iStokphoto; p.11(top right) Doug Berry/iStokphoto; p.11(bottom) Monkey Business Images/Shutterstock; p.12 Bonnie Jacobs/iStockphoto; p.13(left) Mandy Godbehear/Shutterstock; p.13(right) Sean Locke/iStockphoto; p.14(top) Mandy Godbehear/Shutterstock; p.14(bottom) Shutterstock p.15 Guillermo Trejos/iStockphoto; p.16 Skyhawk911/Dreamstime.com; p.17(top left) Orangeline/Dreamstime; p.17(top right) Glenda M. Powers/Shutterstock; p.17(bottom) Jut/Shutterstock.com;p.18 Kamil Cwiklewski/iStockphoto; p.19 Naluwan/iStockphoto; p.20(top) Marc Piscotty/Icon SMI/Newscom; p.20(bottom) Christian Carroll/iStockphoto; p.21(left) Clearviewimages/iStockphoto; p.21(right) Rich Legg/iStockphoto; p.22 Akihiro Sugimoto/AFLO/Newscom; p.23(top) Monkey Business Images/Shutterstock; p.23(bottom) Nattika/Shutterstock; p.24 Nancy Hixson/Shutterstock; p.24(center) Malota/Shutterstock;p.25(left) Sebastian Kaulitzki/Shutterstock; p.25(right) Nathan Gleave/iStockphoto; p.26(top left) Shutterstock; p.26(top right) Bill Fehr/Shutterstock; p.26(bottom) Ruzanna/Shutterstock; p.27 Ranplett/iStockphoto; p.29(all) Nicolle Rager Fuller; p.32(top left) Joyce N. Boghosian, White House photographer; p.32(bottom right) Shutterstock; Back cover Joshua Hodge Photography/iStockphoto

---

Teacher Created Materials
5301 Oceanus Drive
Huntington Beach, CA 92649-1030
http://www.tcmpub.com

ISBN 978-1-4333-3090-2

Printed in Malaysia.
Thumbprints.42806

Table of Contents

Why Should You Play Sports?

You can play basketball, go swimming, play soccer, or dance. You can play baseball, practice karate, play hockey, or run track. There are so many sports to choose from! It can be hard to figure out which sports are right for you. But it can also be healthy and fun! Playing sports can help you build a strong body and get fit.

Learning and playing a sport does even more for your body and mind. You learn new skills. You can learn to hit a ball or make a basket. You make new friends. You learn how to be part of a team. Playing sports can make you feel better about yourself, too. And sports are exciting! But more than anything else, playing sports is fun!

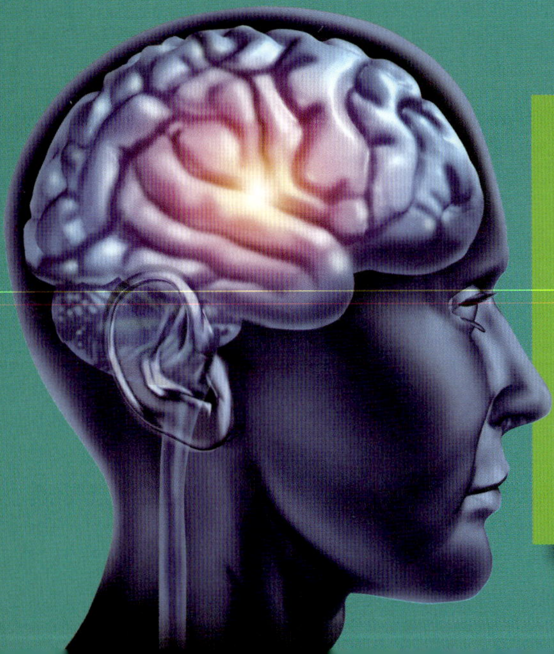

Fun Fact

Scientists have found that exercise can help your body create new brain cells. So when you are building up your **muscles**, you are also building up your brain!

Sports Make You Smarter

Kids who play sports do better in school. That is because being active helps you **concentrate**. It also improves your memory.

Team Sports

Playing with your friends can be great. And what better way to play than on a team? Being part of a team means working together with others to reach a goal. You should not only think of yourself. You need to think of what is best for the whole team. It takes time and practice to work well as a team.

Imagine that you are on a basketball team. Everyone has a position. You might be good at passing the ball. But, you might not ever score a point. That is okay. You are still important to the team's success. And if you are not an expert player, so what! Playing can be fun anyway, if you let it be. And practice will make you better.

Did You Know?

Kids in three out of four U.S. homes play sports. That is 40 million kids!

Why Do Kids Play Sports?

Kids say the top three reasons why they play sports are:

1. To have fun.
2. To make friends.
3. To learn how to play the sport better.

Winning is not why most kids like to play sports. "To win" came in at number 9!

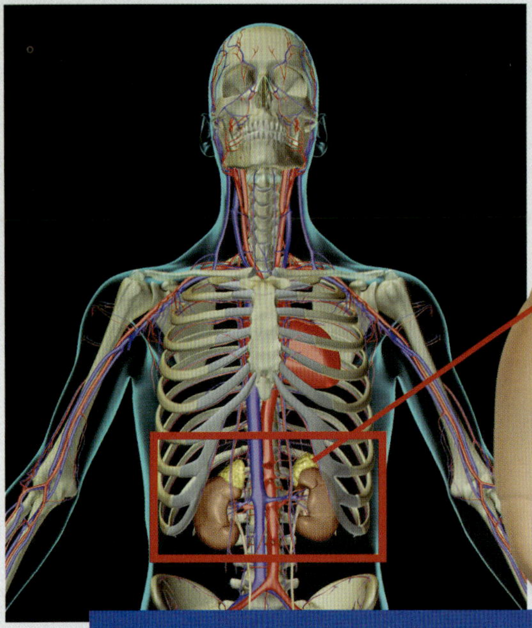

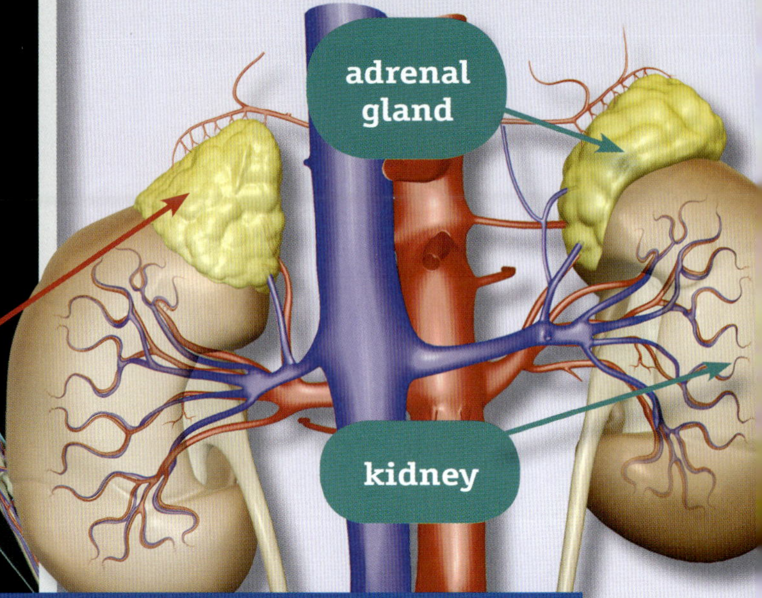

Power Boost

This odd-looking thing on top of the kidney is the adrenal gland. It is small but mighty! The adrenal gland makes **adrenaline** (uh-DREN-ul-in). Adrenaline gives you the **energy** to think and move quickly.

Got Butterflies?

Do you ever get nervous before a big game? Or maybe before you speak in front of your class? That nervous feeling is sometimes called having "butterflies." That is because it feels like you have butterflies fluttering in your stomach. This feeling is just your body making a special chemical called a **hormone**. The hormone it creates is adrenaline. Adrenaline gives your body more energy and gets you ready to perform.

Time to Shine!

There are many team sports. Many kids play baseball, soccer, basketball, or football. Others play volleyball, softball, hockey, or cheerleading.

There are also team sports that let you shine on your own. Think of sports like swimming, and track and field. You can practice and compete on your own with these sports. But you still get to be part of a team. This is a great fit for some kids.

Gymnastics is another example. You can do this sport on your own. Or, you can join a team. Each gymnast on a team may receive a score for his or her skills on the balance beam. But that score may also be a part of a team score. The team can only do well if it is a group effort.

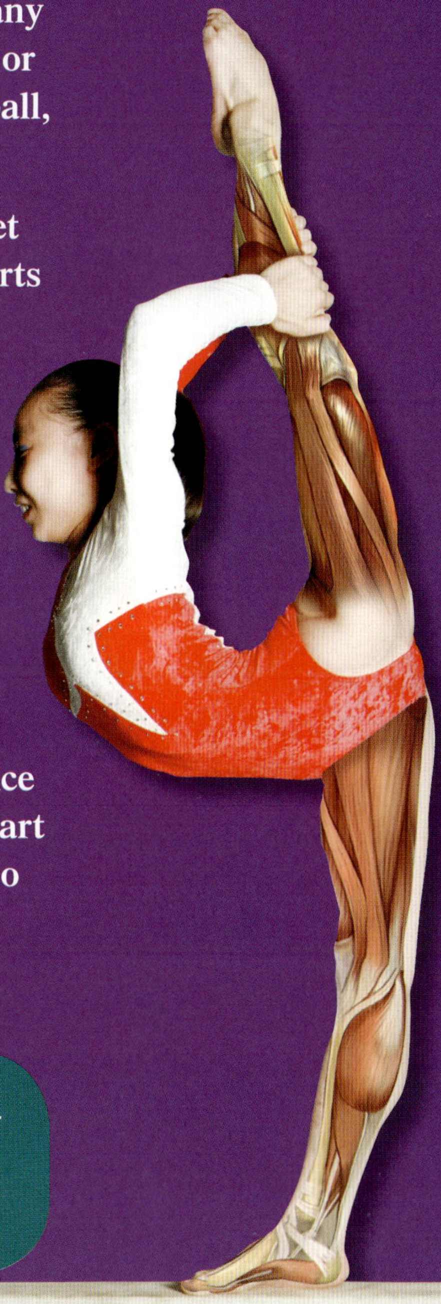

Stretching regularly over time can help make your muscles **flexible.** Flexible means your muscles can stretch and bend easily.

Get in the Game

Starting a new sport can be scary at first. There are new skills and new rules to learn. It may seem like everyone knows more than you. There are things you can do to change this. You could read a book or watch a video to learn about the sport. You could also ask your friends for some tips to help you play the game.

If you are not a new player, you can help others who are. You could offer to explain the rules or even practice with them.

Being on a team can be fun. But it might not always be. Sometimes, sports get very **competitive**. Some coaches, parents, and even teammates may focus too much on winning. They may even yell when someone makes a mistake. You should not take this personally. Just do your best. It is okay to make mistakes. Playing sports is about having fun and learning. Mistakes are part of learning. It takes a long time to become good at a sport. Just keep practicing!

Feeling Stressed?

Are you feeling too much pressure from everyone around you or even yourself? Stress can make your heart race, and can make you nervous and anxious. Too much stress can hurt your body and mind. If you feel stressed, take a few deep breaths and get some light exercise to relax and clear your head.

Be a Good Sport

When two teams compete, there can be only one winner. That means that someone has to lose. Nobody likes to lose. But one of the most important lessons to learn in life is how to deal with your feelings when you lose. It is okay to feel sad or mad. It is not okay to lose your temper, even if you think the game was not fair. Remember, it is only a game.

What you *should* do is congratulate the winner. Give them a high-five or a handshake. People will look at you with respect. They will call you a "good sport." And you will feel good about yourself. That makes you a winner!

Ways to Be a Good Sport

Be a Team Player	Make sure you show up on time for practices and games. Your teammates are counting on you!
Play Fair	Cheating is never okay. Respect the rules of the game.
Be Polite	Saying mean things to the other team is never okay—even if they do it first.
Do Not Point Fingers	Do not ever blame a teammate for messing up. How would it feel if you were in his or her shoes?
Be Respectful	Listen to your coach's directions. Never argue with an official, even if you do not agree with a call.
Be a Graceful Winner	Your team may be cheering, but keep in mind that the other team does not feel so great. Do not **gloat**. And make sure you thank them for playing a good game.

Practicing a sport trains your body to be the best it can be.

Practice, Practice

If you enjoy a sport, one of the best ways to get better is to practice on your own. If you play basketball, see how many baskets you can sink in a row. If you are a dancer, put on some music and practice your moves!

Stick with It

Sometimes you need to be a good sport to yourself. Maybe you joined a team and did not like it. Maybe there were too many practices. Or the coach yelled too much. Try talking calmly with your coach. Ask for tips on how to improve. Or, find another team and coach that are more helpful. Stand up for yourself and do what is best for you.

Do not let one bad experience make you give up on a sport. Give it another try! A great coach and support from your teammates can make all the difference!

Go Solo!

Some sports do not require being on a team at all. You can do them just for fun or to learn new skills. Some of these sports are:

- ✔ Ice skating
- ✔ Running
- ✔ Martial arts
- ✔ Gymnastics
- ✔ Biking
- ✔ Skateboarding
- ✔ Dancing
- ✔ Bowling
- ✔ Golf

Safety First

No matter how much you practice, you may still get hurt. There is a risk of getting hurt no matter what sport you play. Getting an **injury** is no fun. For one thing, it hurts! And you will also likely be out of the game until you have healed. That is no fun, either.

Safety should be your number one priority. You should always be aware of your actions. Try to stay safe. Talk to your friends about making safe choices, too. Do not give in to peer pressure if you know something is dangerous.

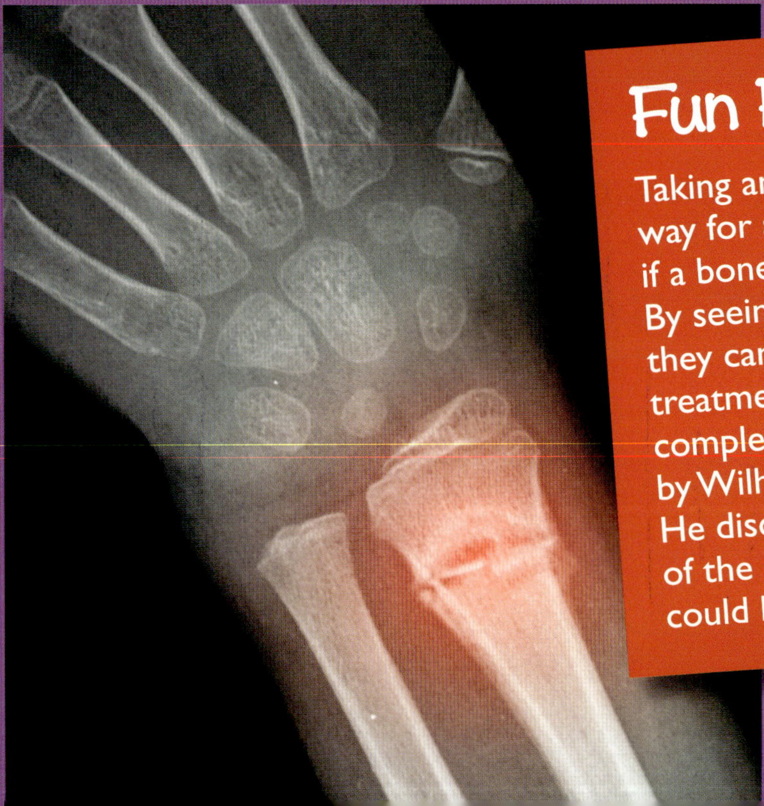

Fun Fact

Taking an X-ray is the quickest way for a doctor to find out if a bone has been broken. By seeing the broken bone, they can decide on the best treatment. X-rays were found completely by accident in 1895 by Wilhelm Conrad Roentgen. He discovered that photographs of the inside of the human body could be taken with x-rays.

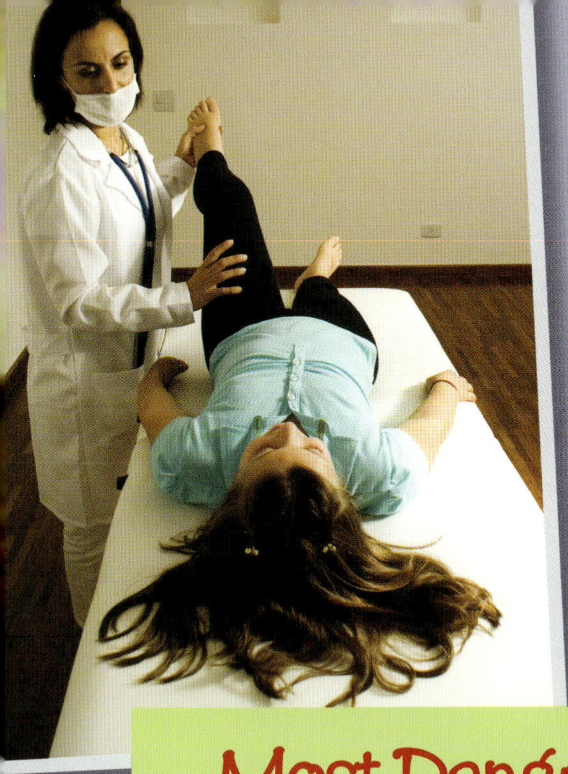

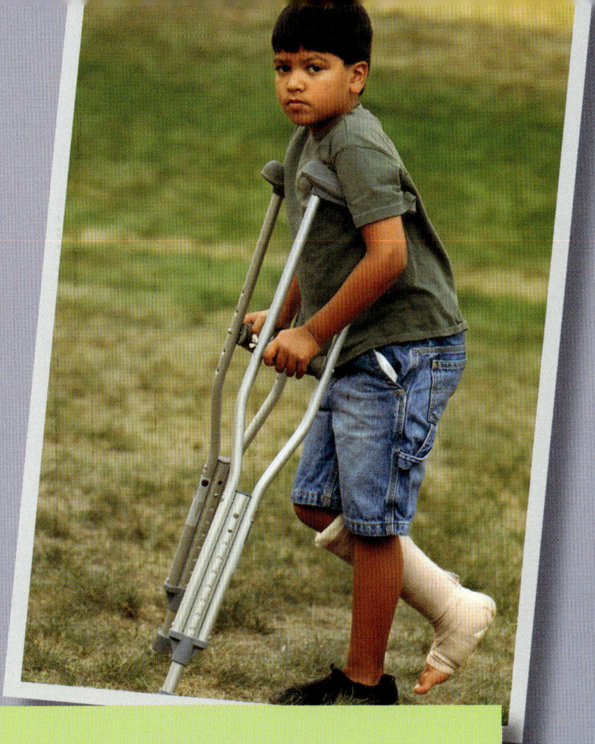

Most Dangerous Sports

A poll of athletes ages 5 to 14 shows the amount of players that were injured playing each sport.

Sport	Percentage of Players Injured
football	28 %
baseball	25 %
soccer	22 %
basketball	15 %
softball	12 %

Preventing Injury

Sometimes you cannot help getting hurt. A fastball might hit you at the plate during a baseball game. Or you may fall off your bike. But there are some things you can do to prevent injuries:

1. **Follow the rules and be aware of your actions.**
   Many kids get hurt because they do not listen to a parent or the coach.

2. **Use safety equipment.**
   You might not like wearing a helmet when you bike. You might not like to wear wrist pads when you skate. But they might be the only things standing between you and a trip to the hospital.

Wear Your Equipment!

You may have noticed that when footba or hockey players put on their uniforms they look bigger. That is because of all the safety equipment they have on underneath their jerseys. This equipmen protects their bodies from injury.

Stretch Your Muscles

A good way to warm up is to stretch your muscles. It will make them more flexible, and increase your blood flow. This can help you avoid getting an injury.

3. Warm up.

Warm up for 5 minutes before you begin an activity. It gets your blood flowing to your muscles. A light jog or jumping jacks will get your blood pumping. Then do some stretches. This will help to prevent muscle injuries.

4. If it hurts, stop!

Stop and rest if any part of your body starts to hurt. Then tell an adult. You might have an injury. You might make it worse if you continue to play.

5. Take a break.

Using the same muscles over and over can cause problems. Give your body some time off each year from your sport. Try something new. You will learn new skills and work other muscles!

Did You Know?

Olympian Shaun White started snowboarding at just 6 years old!

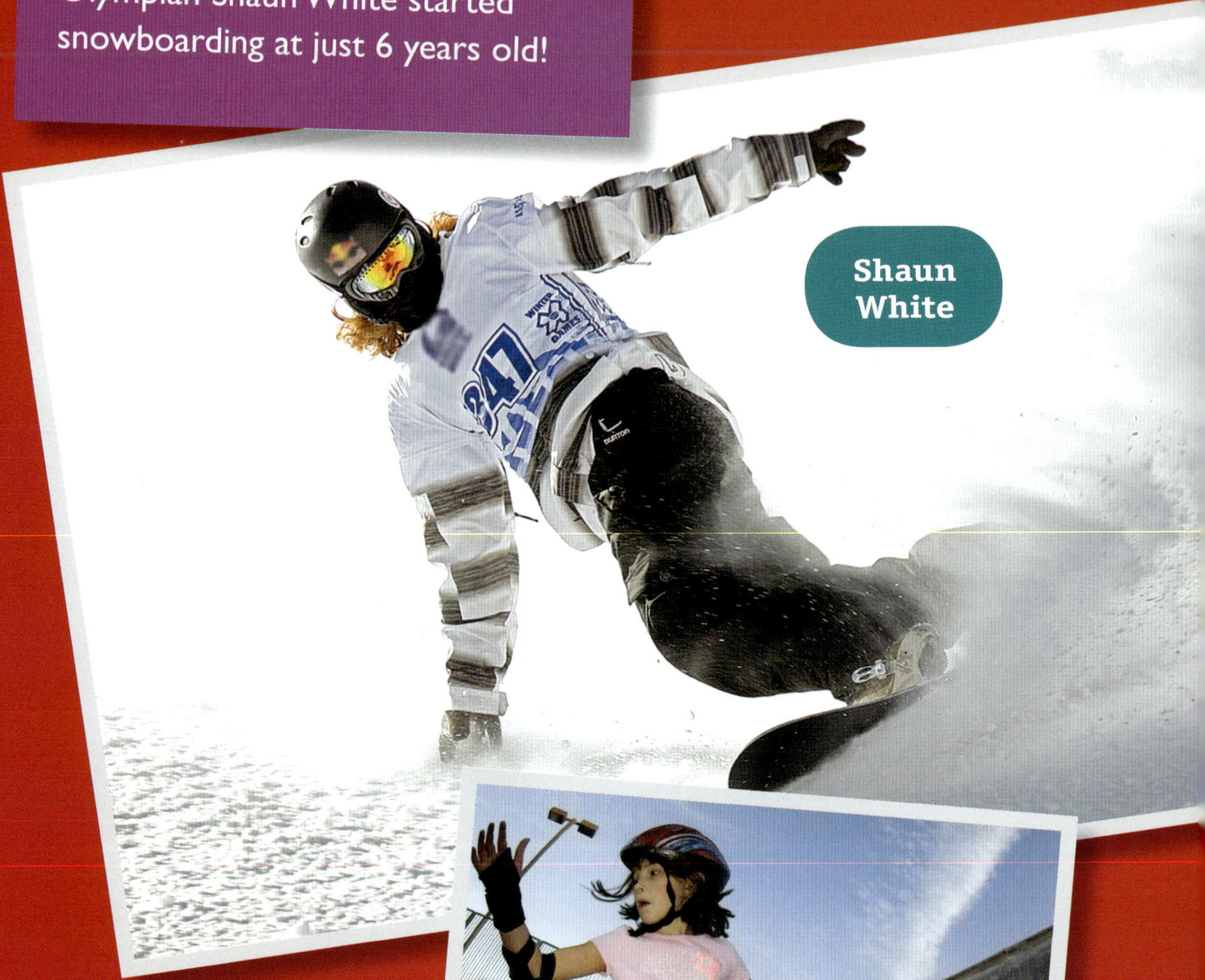

Shaun White

Wear a helmet, knee and elbow pads, and wrist guards to protect yourself from injury.

Extreme Sports? Extreme Safety!

Do you like to push the limits? **Extreme sports** might be for you. Extreme sports are more dangerous than other sports. They can give you an added rush of energy. Skateboarding and off-road biking are extreme sports. Surfing and snowboarding are also extreme sports. Rock climbing is definitely an extreme sport!

These sports look cool. But they can also be risky. That is why it is important always to use the right safety gear. Safety gear will help you practice these sports safely. Wearing the right gear might save you a trip to the hospital.

For many kids, the thrills of these sports are worth the risks. Be sure to check with your parents before practicing an extreme sport.

Eat Like a Champion

You would not ride your bike with two flat tires, would you? Of course not. So then, why would you head out to play without eating healthy foods? Eating the right foods protects your body. It keeps you strong and safe. Your body cannot perform without the right **nutrients** (NOO-tree-uhnts). And your body needs nutrients from a variety of healthy foods. They give you the extra fuel you need to be active.

Good choices to include in your meals are fruits, vegetables, and whole grains. These foods will give you energy. You should also make sure you eat foods with **protein** (PRO-teen). It helps to build and repair muscles. Protein can be found in meat, eggs, cheese, milk, and beans.

Fun Fact

Whether you move or even sit, your body is burning energy. Calories give your body energy. In one day, you should plan to eat as many calories as you burn, or fewer. Most children need somewhere around 2,000 calories a day to be healthy. If you are very active and burn more than that, you may need more calories. Some professional athletes eat food with a total of 4,000 calories a day! They are training hard and need the energy.

Snacks with the Right Stuff

First Lady Michelle Obama has made it her mission to help kids get healthy. One of her tips is to go grocery shopping with your parents. Try some new fruits and vegetables. And read the nutrition labels to find out which foods are healthiest. When it is your turn to bring snacks to your team's game, think healthy!

Instead of Bringing:	Try Bringing:
chips	pretzels, granola bars, or trail mix
candy and cookies	orange slices, apples, watermelon, or dried fruit
soda and sugary juices	water or 100 percent fruit juice
doughnuts	bagels with peanut butter

Do Not Wait Until You Are Thirsty!

Do you sweat when you play outside? That is your body losing water. Your body needs you to replace that water, and quick! So, take regular water breaks. By the time you feel thirsty, you may already be suffering from **dehydration** (dee-high-DRAY-shun). That means your body does not have enough water to work right. Being dehydrated can make you very sick.

You should drink lots of water every day. You need extra water when you are active. You need even more when it is hot outside!

Warning Signs

Here are some signs that you might be getting dehydrated:

- Feeling thirsty
- Feeling dizzy or tired
- Dry lips and mouth
- Rapid heartbeat

Why Does Sweat Stink?

Sweating cools you down when your body gets too hot. But if sweat is mostly water, then why does it smell so bad? Well, it is not really the sweat that smells. What makes it stinky is when it mixes with the **bacteria** (bak-TEER-ee-uh) on your skin. This is another reason to bathe every day with soap and water!

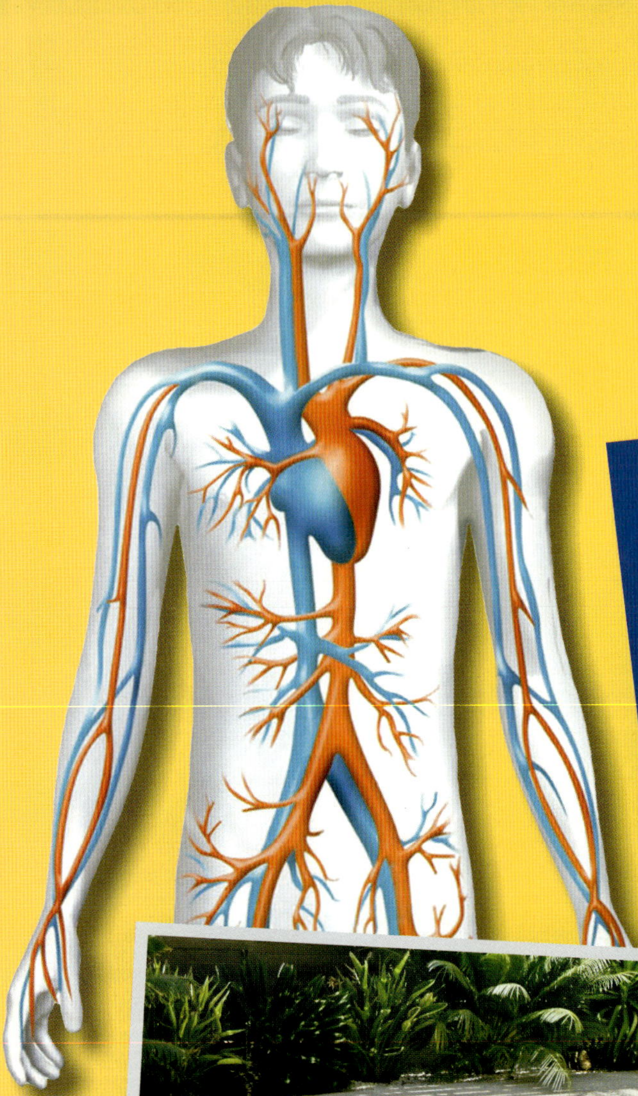

Did You Know?

Your heart is the hardest-working muscle in your body! Every day, your heart beats about 100,000 times. That is enough to pump over 7,500 liters (2,000 gallons) of blood. That much blood could fill a small backyard swimming pool.

Time To Be Active!

So, are you ready to give a new sport a try? Will you join a team? Or, will you try a sport that you can do on your own? Maybe there is a sport you already love and you want to work on getting better at it. The important thing is that you are active. Along with eating right, being active helps you to stay healthy. It makes your heart stronger and builds muscles. It helps you do better in school. Being active even makes you happier!

Need more reasons to get active? When you play sports as a kid, there is a better chance you will be active when you grow up. And active adults lead longer, healthier lives. So get moving!

Lab: Check Your Pulse

Checking your pulse is important when you exercise. It can tell you if you are working your heart too hard or not enough.

Materials

- stopwatch or watch that counts seconds
- sheet of paper
- plastic hoops
- miniature beanbags
- 12 miniature plastic cones

Check Your Pulse

1. Place your index and middle finger on the side of your neck. Move your fingers around until you can feel your blood pulsing. It should feel like a steady beat.
2. Use a stopwatch or a watch with a second hand to take your pulse. Count how many beats you feel in 10 seconds.
3. Multiply the number of beats by 6. That will tell you your heart rate, or pulse, for each minute. A normal heart rate when you are resting is 60 to 100 beats per minute. When you exercise, your target heart rate should be around 175 beats per minute.

Exercise Can Be Fun

4. Check your pulse before exercising. It should be within the normal range. Record your pulse on a sheet of paper.

5. Pair up with a partner and toss a beanbag back and forth while one of you spins a plastic hoop. Keep going until someone drops the beanbag or the hoop. If your team lasts the longest, you win!

6. Check and record your pulse. Is your pulse close to the exercise target range? Is your heart working too hard or not enough?

7. Create two identical obstacle courses using plastic cones. Form teams and have each team member race through the course and back. The fastest team wins! Race again and have players hop through the course or walk backwards.

8. Check and record your pulse again. Has your heart rate changed?

9. Rest for a few minutes and check your pulse again. Is your heart rate returning to normal?

1

7

8

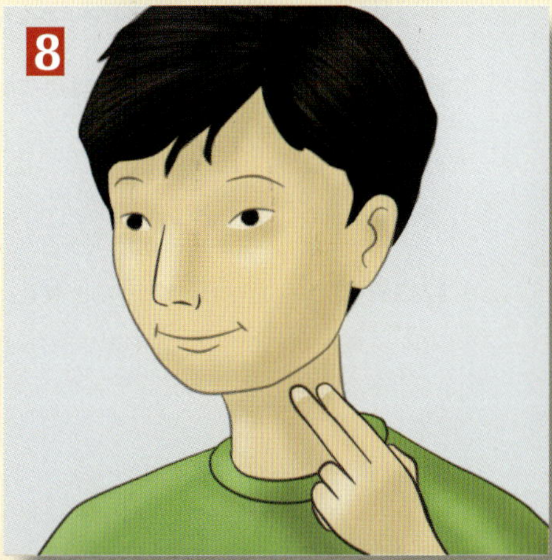

Glossary

adrenaline—a hormone made by your body in response to stress

bacteria—a single-celled organism that can be found on and in our bodies; some types of bacteria are good for us, while others are harmful

competitive—working hard to win

concentrate—to focus on a task

dehydration—the state in which the body has lost too much water to function properly

energy—power or ability to be active

extreme sports—risky activities that involve speed, height, and stunts

flexible—easily bent or stretched in any direction

gloat—to brag or be boastful; to think about something with too much satisfaction

gymnastics—a sport that focuses on strength, balance, and agility performed on or with special equipment

hormone—a chemical in the body that tells it how to work and grow

injury—damage that occurs to part of the body

muscles—tissues in the body that cause movement

nutrients—vitamins, minerals, protein, carbohydrates, fat, and fibers that the body gets from food

protein—a substance found in meat, beans, and nuts that helps build up the tissues in your body

Index

The First Lady's Challenge

She became America's First Lady, but Michelle Obama also had a career in law. That was before she met the future president. In 2008, she and President Barack Obama made history. They became the first African American president and First Lady. They have two daughters. Their names are Sasha and Malia.

Mrs. Obama's role as a mom made her want to help America's children get fit. So she launched a program called *Let's Move!* This program is designed to get kids to be active. So, shut off the TV and computer and go out to play. Ride your bike! Go for a walk! Play a game of tag! Roller skate or skateboard! Mrs. Obama knows that kids who are active and eat healthy foods will grow up to be healthy adults.

Personal Challenge

Check out more about the *Let's Move!* program at **www.letsmove.gov**. Another great program is the *Presidential Champions* program. You can choose from a variety of activities. Then track your progress along the way. Your goal is to see how many points you can earn by being active. Work hard enough, and you can earn a gold medal! Take the *President's Challenge* at **www.presidentschallenge.org**.